BALTHAZAR THE GREAT

Kirsten Sims

Frances Lincoln
Children's Books

Balthazar was *the world's* GREATEST violin-playing polar bear!

These days he was the only violin-playing polar bear left in all the world's circuses. He missed his home, but most of all he missed his grandpa, who had given him his first violin.

One night,

Balthazar was

set free!

He could go home at last.

As long as he could figure out where that was...

"Home must be around here
somewhere," he thought.

But somewhere was a very big place.

Balthazar said GOODBYE to old friends.

And tried to make new ones.

He met others who were looking for home, too.

Some days were happy days.

But sometimes Balthazar felt more *LOST* and lonely than ever.

He was beginning to think
his journey would never end.

But just as he was about to turn back...

...he saw a familiar face.

Could it REALLY be...?

GRANDPA BALTHAZAR!

Balthazar was finally HOME!

And he felt GREATER than ever.